Daisy Punkin

Daisy Punkin

Hilda Stahl

CROSSWAY BOOKS • WHEATON, ILLINOIS
A DIVISION OF GOOD NEWS PUBLISHERS

Daisy Punkin

Copyright © 1991 by Hilda Stahl.

Published by Crossway Books, a division of
Good News Publishers, Wheaton, Illinois 60187.

Cover Illustration: Deborah Huffman

Series design: Ad Plus

First printing, 1991

Printed in the United States of America

Library of Congress Cataloging-in-Publication Data
Stahl, Hilda.
   Daisy Punkin / Hilda Stahl
      p.   cm.
   Summary: Learning about Jesus helps Daisy adjust to her new
school and her mother's temporary absence.
   [1. Family life—Fiction. 2. Schools—Fiction. 3. Christian
life—Fiction.] I. Title.
PZ7.S78244Dai 1991   [Fic]—dc20   91-4693
ISBN 0-89107-617-4

99		98		97		96		95		94		93		92		91
15	14	13	12	11	10	9	8	7	6	5	4	3	2	1

*Dedicated with love to my Punkin
Brittany Elaine Stahl*

Contents

Going Away

1

*D*aisy wanted to grab Momma's hand and hold on tight. But she smiled stiffly and stood at the front door beside Momma. Momma held her worn brown suitcase in one hand and her old brown purse in the other. Daisy's four big brothers stood silently across the small living room beside the couch where Daddy sprawled.

They were all dark like Momma. Daisy was blonde and blue-eyed like Daddy. Daisy said, "You really goin' south, Momma?"

"Sure am, Sugar," Momma shivered and said in her southern drawl. "And I'm glad! I'm not made for this cold Michigan weather. I'm a southern girl, and my blood's too thin." Her eyes darkened even more. She flipped back her long dark hair. "And Nana needs me."

Daisy locked her icy hands behind her back. Maybe Momma would decide to stay once she got there. Daisy's heart jerked. A tight lump almost closed her throat. "Take good care of Nana, Momma."

She nodded and smiled weakly. "I will, Daisy Punkin."

Dad lazily pushed himself up from the couch and rubbed a hand over the tee shirt that Momma kept white. He hiked up the faded jeans that Momma kept patched. "Faye, you tell your momma she's taking you away from your family. And the Christmas tree ain't down yet."

Momma's jaw tightened. "Ed, you know

your sister said she'd come take care of you all the two weeks I'll be gone. Janet said she don't mind a bit."

Daisy glanced at her brothers. They didn't seem any happier than Daddy about Aunt Janet coming.

Momma bent down to Daisy. Daisy smelled Momma's perfume that she used only when she was going somewhere special. "You'll like Aunt Janet, Daisy Punkin. You'll see."

"She's a religious nut," snapped Dad.

Momma kissed Daisy's pale cheek. "I'm real sorry I can't go to your new school with you tomorrow. But you'll be fine. Just dress nice and brush your hair."

Daisy didn't want to think about another new school. Daddy moved them around so much that she'd gone to four different schools since she'd started kindergarten. Suddenly she didn't want to be home alone with Daddy who acted as if she weren't alive or with her big brothers who constantly teased her.

She didn't want to go to a new third grade and meet a new teacher and a room full of strangers. She touched Momma's blue coat sleeve. "I'll go with you. I want to see Nana. I never got to see her before."

"I know, Daisy Punkin. But she gets out of the hospital tomorrow, and she is too weak to have a little girl runnin' around her house."

"Don't let Momma go, Dad," Bill said. His eyes were big in his white face as he looked at Dad. He was ten years old, almost eleven, and in the fifth grade. Daisy knew he wanted Momma to be with him on the first day of a new school, but he'd never tell anyone.

"She'll be back in two weeks," Dad snapped.

Suddenly deep in her heart Daisy knew that Momma would never be back. The four boys had been too rowdy. Daddy had yelled at Momma for not making them mind. Momma had cried, and Daddy had yelled louder.

"Who'll cook for us?" David asked in his

new deep voice that he was so proud of. He was fifteen and always hungry.

"Daisy's not big enough," said Jim. He was fourteen and also always hungry.

"I can make hot dogs in the microwave," said Ron. He was twelve and could eat a whole pack of turkey dogs in one meal.

"We'll get along just fine," Dad said with an impatient wave of his work-roughened hand. "If your momma wants to run off for a rest she don't need before the Christmas tree is even took down, then I say, let her."

Momma's jaw tightened. Her dark eyes flashed. She walked out the door and never looked back.

Daisy ran out after her. Snow covered the small front yard, but the sidewalk was clean. Momma had swept it off early this morning before she'd made breakfast. Tears ran down Daisy's cheeks. "Bye, Momma!"

Momma didn't look back. She didn't wave. She didn't say, "See ya soon, Daisy Punkin."

Daisy watched Momma walk toward the

gas station where the bus stopped. Daisy shivered. Cold on her skin met with the ice in her heart.

"Oh, Momma," she whispered. She slowly stepped back inside. She heard the others in the kitchen arguing over who got the last sugar cookie. She walked to the Christmas tree and touched a jar lid that she'd decorated with green felt and some gold glitter. Momma had said it was beautiful.

Daisy sniffed and blinked back tears. Somehow the box of Christmas decorations had gotten lost the last time they'd moved. Daddy said there wasn't money to buy foolish decorations, so Daisy and Momma had made them.

"Come back, Momma," Daisy whispered.

Daisy heard the others scrape chairs back from the table, and she knew they'd be in to watch Sunday afternoon TV. She ran to her tiny room and closed the door so they wouldn't see her cry.

Later she trudged slowly to the living room.

Daddy was gone. David, Jim, and Ron were watching a war movie on TV, and Bill lay on his stomach coloring a map of the United States. Daisy swallowed hard. Maybe he'd show her the South. She sank down beside him. "Where's Michigan, Bill?"

He scowled at her and then jabbed at Michigan that he'd colored green.

"Where's the South?" she whispered.

"That's a dumb question," he snapped.

She locked her hands over her knees. She could feel the patch that Momma had stitched on the left knee. The jeans were almost too small, but she had only one other pair to use for school. "Where does Nana live?"

"Mississippi," said Bill in a voice that made Daisy know he thought she was really stupid.

Daisy took a deep breath. She knew Bill would get mad, but she had to know. "Where's Mississippi?"

Bill shook his head. "Any dummy knows that."

15

David turned from the TV. "You didn't know it when you were in third grade, Billy."

"Well, I know it now!" He jabbed the map. "Here's Michigan. And here's Mississippi. Now, don't bother me again."

She scooted back, but she kept her eyes glued to the map.

❤ ❤ ❤

First Day

2

*D*aisy slowly hung her red and white jacket that Momma had bought at a yard sale on a hook beside a new blue jacket. She stuck her red mittens in her jacket pockets. Momma had made the mittens for her when the first snow had fallen in November when they'd lived in Lansing. She had begged Momma not to hook them to a string the way kindergarten kids had theirs.

Momma had sighed loud and long. "You're growin' up, Daisy Punkin. You're not my baby girl no more."

"I'm still your baby girl, Momma. I just can't wear mittens hooked to a string. All the kids would laugh at me."

"We can't have no kids laughin' at my baby."

"We can't, Momma."

"Just don't lose them. I don't have no more red yarn since your daddy is on the move again. It'll be a while before we get money for mittens."

"I won't lose them, Momma," Daisy had promised.

She touched her mittens and then pushed them deeper into her pockets. She'd keep them forever — even into fifth grade. She yanked off her dirty white snow boots and pulled up her blue socks — the same ones she'd worn yesterday. She slipped on her worn sneakers and tied the dirty laces. Momma's friend in Lansing had given them to her when her daughter Peggy had outgrown them.

Boys and girls laughed and talked and pushed and shoved all up and down the endless hallway. Smells of wet jackets and coffee from the teachers' lounge hung in the air.

Daisy touched the satiny pink ruffled Christmas dress that Momma had made her. She knew she looked beautiful. Momma had said so when she'd tried the dress on.

Slowly Daisy walked down the crowded hallway to the third grade room. She had asked at the office, and they'd told her she would be in Miss Liscomb's class in Room 110. Her pink dress swished around her knees. Butterflies fluttered in her stomach. She walked into the room and over to Miss Liscomb's tidy desk. Behind her the third graders giggled and whispered.

"Would you look at that dress with those shoes?"

"Does she ever brush her hair?"

Daisy's face flamed. She had forgotten to brush her hair!

She wanted to run from the room. She wanted Momma.

Miss Liscomb looked at her and smiled. Big hoop earrings almost touched her slender shoulders. "You must be Daisy Warren, our new girl from Lansing."

Daisy nodded.

"Welcome to my class. I'm Miss Liscomb. You may sit in that empty seat. You'll learn the rules of my class as we go along." Miss Liscomb's blue eyes sparkled as she smiled again.

Daisy crept to her seat with her head down. She heard more whispers about her dress, but she held back the tears that burned her eyes. She didn't look up when Miss Liscomb introduced her to the class. She tried not to listen as the boys and girls excitedly told about their Christmas gifts and what they had done during Christmas vacation. No way would she tell about her miserable Christmas or her two gifts — her pink dress and a new yellow toothbrush.

Miss Liscomb said, "We have something new in our classroom. A wonderful surprise. Look to the back of the room, please. We have a big aquarium with several interesting fish."

Daisy turned her head to look while the others all talked at once.

Miss Liscomb quieted them and continued, "You may go back to look at the fish at any time without asking me as long as your work is finished."

While she talked, Daisy looked up over the aquarium. Her eyes grew big and round. Hanging on the wall was a giant map of the United States. From looking at Bill's map, she knew right where to look for Michigan and for Mississippi. Unless this map was different. She'd almost failed social studies in Lansing. Why hadn't she studied harder?

Oh, she had to look at the giant wall map! She had to see Mississippi! Momma had said she'd reach Nana's today. Daisy bit her lip. How she wanted to be with Momma right now!

Later she walked to the back of the room as if she were going to look at the fish. She knew she hadn't finished her math work sheet, but she just had to look at the map.

A lump as big as the pink reef in the bottom of the aquarium blocked her throat. She looked away from the fish and up at the huge map. Finally she found Mississippi. Momma should've said, "You go south with me, Daisy Punkin. I want you to get to know Nana. She'll love my Daisy Punkin."

Daisy hugged her thin arms across her thin chest. Momma always called her Daisy Punkin. One day she'd asked, "Why do you call me Punkin, Momma?"

Momma had pulled her close. "I guess because it's a southern pet name, Punkin. You don't mind, do you?"

She did mind a little, but right now she needed to hear Momma call her Punkin.

"Punkin. Punkin," whispered Daisy. But it

wasn't the same. Tears filled her eyes. The recess bell rang, and she quickly rubbed them away.

"Recess time, Daisy," said Miss Liscomb.

"Can't I stay inside. And watch the fish?" asked Daisy.

"No, Daisy. Run outdoors and play with the others." Miss Liscomb waited at the door for Daisy. "I know it's a little scary on the first day of a new school. But you'll make friends."

Daisy shot a look around at the third graders crowded at the coat hooks. She would not make friends with them. Not after they'd laughed at her.

A few minutes later Daisy walked outdoors. Snow crunched under her feet. Cold wind blew against her face. She stopped at the corner of the school and slipped behind an evergreen shrub. She rubbed her eyes with the back of her fuzzy red mittens. She gulped great gulps of cold air that burned her lungs.

No. She would not cry.

Isaac

3

"What's wrong, Daisy?"

With a gasp Daisy peeked around the bush. A boy stood there with a worried look on his face. She stepped forward with her chin high. "Nothing's wrong." Her breath hung in the cold air. Shouts and laughter filled the schoolyard.

He looked all around and then back at Daisy. "You hiding from somebody?"

"No."

He pushed his hands into his jacket pockets and smiled. "Do you know who I am?"

She frowned. "No."

"Isaac Griffin. I sit behind you."

"Oh." Now she remembered. He was the boy who always had the answers to everything, and he always had them right. His clothes looked neat and clean. He'd tried to talk to her a few times, but she hadn't answered him.

He peered closer at her. "How come you're so sad?"

Daisy froze. "Who says I am?"

"I do."

"Well, I'm not."

"Yes, you are."

"So?" She scowled at him to try to make him leave, but he stood there as if to say her scowls didn't bother him.

He rubbed the toe of his boot across a

clump of dirty snow. It left a wide line. "It makes me feel bad to see you sad."

She trembled. "Why don't you leave me alone?"

"I can't."

"You can!"

He shook his head, and she thought maybe *he* was going to cry. "I can't," he said again.

"Why not?"

He looked all around and then whispered, "Because I love you."

"What?" The word shot from her mouth.

"I do."

Fire flashed from her blue eyes. "You do not!"

"Yes, I do."

"You can't."

"I do."

She looked helplessly around. She saw girls on the swing. A group of boys were throwing snowballs at each other even though they weren't supposed to. Finally she faced Isaac. "Leave me alone."

"I didn't tease you about your pink dress."

"So?"

He shrugged again. "I just wanted you to know."

"You don't even know me. I'm new here."

"I saw you walk in today, and you looked pretty and sad and scared."

Daisy didn't know what to say.

"I tried to talk to you."

"I didn't want anybody to talk to me."

"How come?"

She clamped her mouth closed and shook her head.

He pushed his hat back off his forehead. "You still look sad, and I want to make you feel better."

She moved restlessly. No boy had ever loved her before. Once when they'd lived near Flint, she'd loved Adam Tol. Then they'd moved and she'd stopped loving him. "I don't even know you."

"That's all right," said Isaac. "Once you do, maybe you'll love me back."

She had her doubts. She was too busy thinking about Momma to think about loving anyone.

Isaac leaned toward her. "Want to play on the teeter-totter?"

Daisy shrugged.

"I won't bump it hard."

She looked at his brown face and wide gray eyes and finally nodded. He was a little shorter than she was and just as thin. He wore jeans, black snow boots, and a dark blue jacket with a fuzzy collar. A knitted red cap covered his ears and most of his light brown hair. Finally she nodded.

She walked with him across the schoolyard to the empty teeter-totter. Three boys and a girl ran past. They shouted and kicked up snow. The smell of wood smoke drifted from a chimney of a nearby house.

"Where do you live, Daisy?" asked Isaac.

"On Bender Street. 1283."

"Hey, I know where that is. I live at 1625 Locust."

"We just moved here two days before Christmas, so I don't know where Locust Street is."

"I'll draw you a map." He bent down, pulled a stub of a red pencil out of his pocket, and drew in the snow beside the steel pole that held the teeter board. He told her the names of streets between the school and Bender and Locust. "I live here, and you live right there. If I cut across this yard, I could be at your house in two minutes and we could play. Do you like to play hockey?"

"Some."

"Soccer?"

"Yes." She sat on the teeter board while he sat on the opposite end. They went up and down. Isaac talked about things he liked to do. She told him some of the things she liked to do. Not once did she talk about Momma. When the bell rang, he eased off the board and held it until she slid off.

"Meet you at lunch, and we'll eat together," he said.

She nodded.

Just as she reached the back of the line of boys and girls, he stepped closer to her and whispered, "Do you love me yet?"

"No."

"That's okay." He smiled and ran to hang up his jacket.

A few minutes later, she walked back into the classroom. Her cheeks were red from cold. Her fingers felt numb. The room seemed hot and stuffy. She glanced at Miss Liscomb standing at her desk talking to a group of girls. Daisy took a deep breath. She walked fast to the back of the room to study the wall map again. Just how many miles was it from Michigan to Mississippi?

"What're you looking at, Daisy?"

She jumped at the sound of Isaac's voice. She leaned her head close to his. His light brown hair stood on end from when he'd pulled off his red cap. "How far is Michigan from Mississippi?" she whispered.

He studied the map in deep concentration

and then looked at her closely. "Are you going to Mississippi?"

Was she? She didn't know yet. "I might."

"I hope you don't."

"I might not."

"Why do you want to go to Mississippi?"

She twisted her fingers together. Should she tell him?

Miss Liscomb clapped her hands together twice. "Take your seats, children. Daisy. Isaac. It's time for reading."

"We'll talk later," whispered Isaac.

Daisy nodded. She walked to her seat, sat down, and pulled out her reading book.

The News

4

*J*ust before science, Daisy walked back to the wall map. She reached up and touched Mississippi. How warm was it there?

Alison, the girl who sat on Daisy's left, waved her hand high. "Miss Liscomb, the new girl is looking at the fish again. She doesn't have her work done yet."

Daisy frowned at Alison. Alison lifted her chin and looked right back at Daisy.

Miss Liscomb walked back to Daisy. "Sit down, Daisy," she said in a low voice. She led Daisy to her desk and leaned down until her huge red hoop earrings almost touched Daisy's shoulder. In a low voice she said, "You must not abuse the privilege of watching the fish, Daisy, even if you're new to us. You finish your work first, and you can look at the fish then. Not before."

"Yes, ma'am," Daisy said just the way Momma had told her people from the South did.

"There'll be time after lunch for you to watch the fish again."

Daisy nodded. Miss Liscomb smiled and walked away. She left a trail of perfume that smelled just like Momma's.

The words in Daisy's science book blurred. She blinked hard and rubbed the back of her hand across her nose. She could not cry and have everyone look at her and call her a baby.

Alison leaned across the aisle and whispered, "Hey, new girl. I hate your pink dress."

Daisy stuck her tongue out at Alison.

Alison waved her hand high. "Miss Liscomb, the new girl stuck her tongue out at me."

Miss Liscomb frowned. "Alison, stop being such a tattletale. Daisy, don't stick your tongue out at Alison."

Daisy ducked her head and wouldn't look up even when Alison whispered to her again.

At lunch Isaac leaned across the narrow table and whispered to Daisy, "Alison is mean."

"She really is," said Daisy. She glanced across the crowded cafeteria where Alison sat with several girls.

"Miss Liscomb stinks," said Isaac.

Daisy shook her head. "No, she doesn't!"

Isaac fingered his plastic fork. "She made me mad by walking you to your seat. You should've told her you wanted to study the map and not watch the fish. Maybe then she would've let you stay there."

"It's all right." Daisy picked at the corndog on the Styrofoam plate. The noise in the cafeteria hurt her head, and she didn't feel much like eating.

Isaac tore open his tiny potato chip bag. "Why do you want to go to Mississippi?"

Before Daisy could answer, a girl dressed in a snagged flowered blue sweater and faded jeans plopped down beside Daisy. She had long, dark hair that needed brushing and dirty hands. Her blue eyes sparkled. "Hi, Isaac. Hi, Daisy. Care if I sit here?" She took a big bite of her corndog.

Daisy looked over at Isaac, then back at the girl.

"We wanted to talk by ourselves, Karen," said Isaac. "But you can sit with us. Right, Daisy?"

"Sure." Daisy stuck her thin red straw into her milk carton.

Karen swallowed her food. "Daisy, I tried to tell you not to watch the fish so much, but you couldn't hear me." Karen jabbed her thin chest with her dirty finger. "I sit closest to the aquarium."

Daisy shrugged. She didn't remember seeing Karen before.

Karen flipped back her tangled hair. "You guys hear about that murdered woman the police found near my house?" Karen beamed at Isaac and then at Daisy. "I bet I'm the only kid in third grade that ever had a murdered woman near her house."

Daisy's stomach tightened. Her hands suddenly felt colder than the tiny cup of vanilla ice cream on her tray. What if Momma had never reached the bus? What if Momma was murdered?

"I didn't hear about it," said Isaac.

"It wasn't anyone my dad knew." Karen sucked on her straw until her mouth was full of milk, and then she swallowed noisily. "My dad went right over and looked at the dead body and everything. He said she was all beat up. The police say somebody dropped her off there. I don't know how they could tell that, but that's what they said."

The room spun. Daisy gripped the seat of her chair with both her hands.

"What's wrong, Daisy?" Karen leaned close enough for Daisy to smell her dirty hair and clothes. "Does it make you sick to hear about dead people? I could shut up if you want. Just say so."

Daisy couldn't speak. She wanted to run from the room, but she knew her legs would collapse. She'd sprawl down on the floor while everyone else was eating and laughing and talking.

"Are you all right, Daisy?" asked Isaac with a worried frown.

She barely nodded.

"Are you going to faint?" asked Karen.

Daisy shook her head just enough to let Karen know she wasn't.

"Well, if you are, you tell me, and I'll push your head down between your knees. I saw that on TV, and it worked. You just put your head down between your knees, and then you don't faint." Karen pushed several potato chips into her mouth and crunched down on them. "Daisy, if you don't want your ice cream, I'll eat it."

Daisy pushed it toward her.

Karen took it and flipped off the lid. "Want to share it, Isaac?" asked Karen.

"Sure." He reached over and scooped out part of it and dropped it in his ice cream container.

"I can't eat any more," said Daisy in a choked voice. "You can have the rest of my stuff."

"Are you sick or something?" asked Karen. She grabbed up the corndog.

"No, just not hungry." Daisy saw the questions in Isaac's eyes, but she didn't want to answer them. She slipped out of her chair and walked out of the noisy room to the bathroom. Weakly she leaned against the cool green tile. "It can't be Momma. She can't be dead," she whispered. Her hands shook. Tonight she'd watch the news, and she'd know for sure. Finally she pushed away from the wall. She walked out just as several girls walked in.

The day dragged, but finally it was almost time to leave. Miss Liscomb stood at her desk and smiled. Her blonde curls bounced as she walked around her desk. Her bright eye makeup looked as fresh as it had this morning.

"Class, how many of you like to watch commercials on TV?"

Most of the hands shot up. Daisy lifted hers only halfway up. She liked funny commercials sometimes.

Miss Liscomb smoothed her skirt over her slim hips and touched the red beads hanging on her blouse. "Thursday Jason Silva is coming to talk to us about TV commercials. He writes them. That's how he makes a living. He's going to teach us how to make up commercials, and then we're going to write and produce our own commercials."

Daisy sat with her icy hands in her lap while the others clapped. She couldn't think about commercials. At six o'clock she'd watch the news for the story about the murdered woman.

❤ ❤ ❤

Unexpected Visitor

5

Daisy stepped through her back doorway. She pulled off her red mittens and white boots. Noises came from the kitchen. None of her brothers would be home yet. She shivered. Was it Aunt Janet?

Or could it be Momma?

Daisy's heart leaped. She ran into the small

kitchen, and then came to a dead stop. A strange man dressed in new jeans and a bold gray-green and black sweater was lifting the silverware basket out of the dishwasher. Was he stealing their silverware? Daisy gasped and then clamped her shaking hand over her mouth.

The stranger turned and grinned. His even, white teeth flashed in his sun-darkened face. He was tall and slim. He looked only a few years older than her brother David. He even looked like David. "Hi, ya, Daisy," he said.

Her jacket suddenly felt too hot. "Who . . . who are you?"

"You mean you don't recognize me?" He set the basket on the counter near the silverware drawer and looped his thumbs in his back pockets. His dark hair waved back from his wide forehead. His left ear stuck out from his head a little. "It's not been that long, has it? I saw you when you lived in Mt. Pleasant."

She stood behind a kitchen chair, out of his reach. "I can't remember you."

His twinkling blue eyes crinkled at the corners when he smiled. "I always send you a birthday card with five dollars."

Daisy's heart leaped. "Oh! I know! Cousin Matthew! I can't believe it! Matt! What're you doing here?"

Matt laughed, then sobered. "Mom couldn't come after all. So, I did." He opened a cupboard under the counter, stuck in a pan, and then pushed the door shut with his foot. "I'm helping out while your mom's in Mississippi."

Daisy dropped her jacket on a chair and walked up to Matt. "Are you sure . . . Momma's . . . there?"

"Hey, don't look so scared, Daisy."

Giant tears welled up in Daisy's eyes. "Are you sure?"

Matt dropped to his knee and wrapped his arms around Daisy. She stiffened and then let him hold her. She smelled his after-shave and heard the thump of his heart. Finally he held her away from him and gently pushed strands of her blonde hair out of her pale face. "Of course she's there! Your momma loves you, Daisy. You know that. She had to go help her mom for a while."

Daisy pulled away. "How'd you get in?"

"My mom told me where your mom hid the key."

"Oh." Daisy laced her fingers together. "How come you're not in college?"

"I have another two weeks before I have to go back. I planned to spend extra time with my girlfriend, but she broke up with me." His voice trailed off, and a look of pain crossed his face. Then he smiled again. "So I was glad when Mom asked if I could come in her place."

Daisy looked around the kitchen. It was clean. She looked at the stove. Even that was clean. "Can you cook?"

"Sure."

"And do the laundry?"

"Of course."

"Our boys can't do anything. But fight."

"I used to fight with my brothers too."

Daisy looked at him for a long time. "Does Dad know you're here?"

Matt chuckled and dropped the forks and spoons into the drawer. "He's expecting Mom. But he'll have to settle for me."

Daisy leaned against Matt. "Will Momma ever come home?"

"Of course!"

"Today a girl in my class said that . . . that the police found a . . . a murdered woman."

"Oh, Daisy!" Matt held her close and patted her back as if she were a baby. "To make you feel better, I'll call your mom and you can talk to her."

"Nana doesn't have a phone."

Matt thought for a minute. "Then I'll call the police and see who the murdered woman is."

Daisy's stomach cramped. She knuckled away tears as she walked to the living room with Matt to the only phone in the house. She leaned against the worn couch and watched him find the Honor City Police in the phone book.

He glanced at her and winked.

She held her breath while he told the police why he was calling. Finally he hung up and scooped her up and lifted her high into his arms.

"It wasn't your momma, Daisy."

She laughed right out loud.

The back door slammed.

"The boys are home," she said. She pushed against his wide shoulders to make him put her down.

"Let's go talk to them." Matt held her hand, and together they walked to the kitchen.

The four boys stopped short and stared.

"Matt!" said David and Jim at the same time.

"When did you come?" asked Ron.

Bill didn't say anything as he dropped his books to the table.

Daisy sank to a chair and listened as the boys talked to Matt. The kitchen seemed packed with boys just as it did every evening, only this time they weren't being rowdy.

"What time does your dad get home?" asked Matt.

"At six," said David, glancing at the round clock on the wall in back of the table.

"Then I think we'd better fix supper," said Matt. "All of us will work together."

Daisy's eyes grew big and round as she waited for the boys to argue the way they did when Momma asked for help. But they didn't. Matt told them what to do, and they did it. They hardly ever did what Momma said.

"Daisy, you set the table," said Matt.

She jumped up. Sometimes she didn't do what Momma said either. She took off Bill's books and put the plates around. She stood beside Momma's place and sighed.

"Do you really think Dad'll let you stay?" asked Jim as he chopped the lettuce for a salad.

Matt chuckled. "Mom couldn't come, so I'm all the help he's getting right now since he can't afford to hire someone."

Later when Daisy heard Dad's car in the

drive, she stepped closer to Matt. He didn't seem concerned at all.

Dad walked in, dirty from working at putting heating plants in new buildings. He looked quickly around the suddenly quiet kitchen and then stared at Matt. He scowled. "Where's your mother?"

"She couldn't come, Uncle Ed, so I did."

Dad pulled off his paisley cap, leaving his hair plastered down on the sides and in spikes on top. "You think you're gonna take care of us?"

Daisy wanted to hide in her bedroom, but she sank down on her chair. She locked her fingers in her lap. For once the boys sat in silence at the table.

Matt shrugged. "I can do anything when I have to."

Dad looked at the spaghetti, meatballs with sauce, garlic bread, and a large bowl of tossed salad on the table. He frowned.

"The kids and I did it," said Matt with a grin.

"That's hard to believe." Dad washed his

hands at the kitchen sink, dried on a dish towel, then sat down, and started eating.

"Is it all right if I thank God for the food?" asked Matt.

Daisy peeked at Dad as he nodded, but continued to eat.

Matt bowed his head. "Heavenly Father, thank You for loving this family. Take care of Aunt Faye and her mother. Thank You for this good food. It's blessed in Jesus' name. Amen."

Daisy felt funny inside to have Matt talk to God as if He were real. Matt was the only person she'd ever met who talked about Jesus as if he were a friend instead of a swear word. She glanced at the others. Daddy looked at his plate while he chewed garlic bread. The boys were quiet for once.

"Here you go, Daisy," said Matt.

She took the bowl of spaghetti that he held out to her.

❤ ❤ ❤

Matt

6

*D*aisy wiped off her mouth with the back of her hand. She glanced at Dad. Butterflies fluttered in her stomach. Any minute she expected him to tell Matt to leave and not return. She watched David push back his chair. He looked determined. She saw a spot of sauce at the corner of his mouth.

"I'll be back later," David said. "I'm going to Roger's for a while."

"Hold it," said Matt.

David frowned.

"What about the dishes?" asked Matt.

Daisy blinked in surprise.

"What about 'em?" David rubbed a crumb off his gray sweatshirt.

"We're going to clean the kitchen together." Grinning, Matt jumped up and carried his plate and glass to the sink.

Daisy waited for David to yell in anger, but to her surprise he carried his plate to the sink, scraped it, and loaded it in the dishwasher along with his glass and silverware. The smell of garlic and spaghetti sauce hung heavy in the air.

"You have something red right here, David," said Jim, rubbing the corner of his own mouth.

David wiped off the sauce with a napkin and gave it a basketball toss into the wastebasket.

Daisy peeked at Dad, but his eyes were blank, and she knew he hadn't heard a word. He walked out of the kitchen, and in a minute the TV blared.

"Working together makes things easier," said Matt. "You're all big enough to know that."

"I got homework," said Bill around a bite of garlic bread.

Matt knuckled Bill's head. "You can do it later, Cousin."

Bill jerked away and slipped off his chair. Fire shot from his dark eyes that were so much like Momma's. "You're not my boss . . . Cousin!"

Daisy sat on her hands and held her breath.

Matt looked at Bill calmly. "We all work together, Bill, and that's final."

"Who's gonna make me?" Bill's voice rose. "Momma never made us do nothing."

"Well, she should've," snapped Matt. "You want to turn into some kind of lazy juvenile delinquent? I'm not your slave, and your mother shouldn't be either."

Daisy sank low in her chair.

Jim gripped Bill's arm. "Do what he says, Bill."

Bill jerked away. "I won't!" His voice rang out even louder than the TV.

"Don't be such a fifth grade jerk," yelled Ron.

"Stay out of it, Ron!" snapped David.

Daisy glanced toward the living room. She sucked in her breath at the sight of Dad standing in the doorway. His face looked like a dark thundercloud. His work shirt hung open and down over his jeans.

"What's going on in here?" Dad looked right at Matt. "Are you causing trouble?"

Daisy wanted to run to Matt's side and protect him from Dad's anger, but she stayed where she was.

Matt lifted his chin, and a muscle jumped in his jaw. "Uncle Ed, we are all going to work together to do the work around here. I came to help out, but I will not be a slave."

Like Momma, Daisy thought and then flushed painfully.

"I want Momma home," said Bill, his face set stubbornly.

"Well, she ain't home," snapped Dad. "I worked hard all day, and I'm not gonna listen to fights. Get the job done and leave me in peace!" He walked away, leaving a great silence in the kitchen.

Daisy watched the color drain from Bill's face. He grabbed his plate, dropped it in the dishwasher, and then flung in his fork. Slowly Daisy carried her dishes to the dishwasher. She put the Romano cheese in the refrigerator and the salt and pepper in the cupboard beside the stove while the boys worked in silence beside Matt. The whirl of the water in the dishwasher sounded louder than usual. Once in a while Matt gave a quiet order. Ron finished sweeping the floor and put the broom away.

With a pleased look on his face Matt said, "Well done, gang. And it only took us fifteen minutes."

Daisy slipped her hand in his, and he smiled down at her.

"Now can I go?" asked David with a slight frown.

"In a minute, Dave." Matt smiled at him and then looked at the other boys. "I washed clothes earlier, and I folded them in your bedroom. Sort them and put them away. After that, David, you may go. And, Bill, you may study."

Without their usual yells and wrestling, the boys pushed through the door to go to the bedroom they shared.

"I left your clothes on your bed, Daisy," said Matt. "You go put them away. If you need help, holler."

Daisy walked to the door. Then she ran back to Matt and gripped one of his hands in both of hers. "Matt, if we work real hard, will Momma come back?"

He bent down and kissed the top of her head. "Little Daisy, your momma will come back in two weeks."

But what if Matt was wrong?

Daisy's heart sank. Maybe Momma would never come back.

In her room Daisy dropped down on her unmade bed beside the pile of folded clothes. She looked at the dirty walls that once had been painted blue and down at the worn brown tweed carpet. Momma had said, "Daisy Punkin, if we live here long enough and have the money, we'll paint your room any color you want and maybe get a new carpet. We'll make it a nice room for my little girl."

Daisy held back tears. She whispered, "I don't care how it looks. I just want you back, Momma."

After a long time, Daisy noticed her closet door hung open and her doll and doll clothes lay on the floor beside the sweater she'd worn two days ago. Her stuffed animals lay in a heap in the corner beside her wastebasket. She saw the red dog that she'd slept with since Momma had given it to her, and she looked quickly away.

Slowly she dropped her clothes in her drawers and walked to the window to look out at the snow in the backyard. Three small, gray birds pecked at crumbs that Matt must've tossed out. The neighbor's yard was smooth with snow. No footprints messed it up. The snow in her yard was trampled and dirty.

Finally she turned away from the window and noticed the drawers hanging open on her dresser. A picture of Momma closing her dresser drawers flashed across her mind. With a strangled cry she pushed the drawers shut. A cobweb looped down in the corner near the door, and she flung a rolled-up sock against it to knock it down.

Matt stuck his head in her door. "Go take your shower, Daisy."

"Do I have to?"

"Sure do. With only one bathroom you know we all have to take turns in the shower."

She pushed her hair back. "Who'll comb my wet hair when I'm done?"

"I will."

"Can you comb hair?"

Matt shrugged. "I've never combed a little girl's hair before, but I'm sure I can."

"Momma always combed my hair. She could do it without hurting me."

"I won't hurt you."

Daisy's lip trembled, and she whispered, "I want my momma, Matt."

"I know you do." Matt knelt down and hugged her close. "Let me pray for you."

Daisy slowly nodded.

"Heavenly Father, in Jesus' name help little Daisy. Help her to be patient while her momma is helping Mrs. Bovier. Let her know that You love her even more than her momma does."

Daisy always got a funny feeling inside when Matt said Jesus loved her. She leaned her head against his shoulder. When he finished praying, she asked, "Matt, who's your Heavenly Father?"

"God is."

"Does He hear you when you talk to Him?"

"Yes."

"Does He answer?"

"Yes."

She thought about that, and she snuggled

closer to Matt. Would his Heavenly Father hear and answer this time? Then she had another thought. Could she talk to God like Matt?

At bedtime she curled up on her bed, her flannel pajamas warm and soft against her body. Her blonde hair was dry and pretty. Matt had used the blow dryer on it as he'd combed it, and he'd talked to her about her day at school. She'd told him about Alison and Karen and Isaac. She hadn't told him that Isaac loved her. He might laugh the way her brothers would've.

She glanced across the room at the pile of stuffed animals. Slowly she slipped off the bed and picked up the plush red dog. Momma had given the old red stuffed dog to her when she was five.

Momma had said, "I found it at a yard sale, and I knew you'd love it, Daisy Punkin. What'll you name it?"

Daisy had held the red dog up and looked at the ripped ear and the rubbed-off spots. "Scruffy. No! Scruffy Punkin."

Now Daisy sniffed and rubbed her head against Scruffy Punkin. "I'm sorry I threw you on the floor when Momma left. I was mad 'cause I wanted to go with her. But I couldn't go." Daisy kissed Scruffy Punkin's nose. "Did you miss me today? I missed you something awful!" She squeezed Scruffy Punkin tighter. "I want Momma," she whispered so the boys wouldn't hear and call her a baby.

A tear ran down the side of her face and soaked into Scruffy Punkin. She reached to rub it away and felt something sharp. She saw a piece of white paper tucked under the red ribbon around Scruffy Punkin's neck. Her heart beat faster. Her hand trembled as she pulled out the paper. Slowly, awkwardly, she opened it. Her nerves danced. "A note," she whispered. The printed words blurred as her eyes filled with tears. "It's a note from Momma."

❤ ❤ ❤

The Note

7

With her foot Daisy closed her bedroom door quietly. Her room was so small that she could touch both her bedroom door and closet door without moving off her single bed. The boys' room was big enough to hold two sets of bunk beds and a big dresser with two feet of floor space left. Momma and Dad's room was crowded with their queen-size bed.

Daisy's head spun as she looked at the note again. She hadn't dreamed it. Momma had hidden a note for her in Scruffy Punkin! It was for her alone, not for the boys and not for Dad.

She read in a whisper, "My sweet Daisy Punkin, I love you. I will miss you a lot while I am gone. You be a good girl for Aunt Janet. Mind her and don't sass back. Let her teach you about God. She says if we all loved Jesus, we would have a happy family. I know that you are sometimes as unhappy as me. See you in a few days. Love, Momma."

A note from Momma!

Daisy pressed the note to her heart and laughed under her breath. She picked up Scruffy Punkin and squeezed him tight. "Listen to this, Scruffy Punkin!" She read the note in a whisper to her red dog. "Momma will see me in a few days!"

She read the note again. "I never knew Momma was unhappy." Daisy remembered a few days ago when Momma had cried and yelled at Dad because they didn't have money for Christmas gifts.

Once again Daisy read the note; then over and over she read the words, "My sweet Daisy Punkin, I love you."

The words warmed her for a minute and then left her shivering. Daddy would never, ever want them to love Jesus, but since Momma wanted them to, Daisy wanted to love Him.

Just then someone knocked and she jumped. In a flash she stuffed the note under her pillow and said, "Come in."

Matt walked in. He looked tired, but he smiled. "Want to come have a snack in the kitchen with me and the boys?"

She thought of the note. She wanted to read it again.

"Jim's making popcorn," said Matt.

Just then the smell reached her, and she breathed deeply. "It does smell good." She thought about the note hidden under her pillow. Should she show it to Matt?

"What's wrong, Daisy?"

She jumped and felt the heat rush over her neck and face.

"Nothing. I want some popcorn. Do we have any orange pop?" She laid Scruffy Punkin on her pillow right over the note and walked out with Matt.

"No, we have only water to drink."

The TV was quiet for once, and Daisy noticed Dad wasn't in his chair where he always sat to watch.

"Your dad went out," said Matt. "He didn't tell us where he was going or when he'd be back."

Daisy shrugged. It didn't matter to her. Some kids told stories about doing things with their dads, but she'd always thought they'd made up the stories. Only dads on TV or in books did fun things together with their families.

In the kitchen Daisy filled a bowl with popcorn and sat on her chair to eat the hot, buttery kernels. For once the boys weren't fighting.

"Matt, you said you'd tell us about your girlfriend," said David as he sprinkled cheese on his popcorn.

Matt sighed heavily. "We broke up. She said she wanted to date someone else."

"Just like a girl," said Jim. "Me and Gina were going together when we lived in Lansing. She broke up just because some guy gave her a bouquet of balloons."

Daisy remembered how upset Jim had been when he'd told Momma about Gina.

"There are other girls, Jim," Momma had said, and Jim had run to his room and wouldn't talk to her for a long time after that.

"There's an eighth grade girl I like," said Ron as he leaned back against the sink. "But she won't look at me since I'm only in seventh grade."

"Who is it?" asked Jim. "I might know her."

"Belinda. I don't know her last name. She's blonde and tall, taller than me."

"Who's not?" David nudged Matt and laughed.

Ron frowned at David before he turned back to Jim. "Today she wore a long pink sweater, jeans, and high-heeled shoes."

"Sure. Belinda Zolta. She's pretty, but her parents don't let her go with boys yet."

Daisy listened as David, Jim, and Ron continued to talk with Matt about girls. She glanced at Bill. He wasn't interested in girls yet, or he wouldn't admit to it. He sat at the table with his homework while he pushed popcorn into his mouth with one hand and scribbled on his paper with the other. Once in a while he looked up as the boys talked and laughed. He never said a word. Sometimes Daisy wondered what he thought about.

Daisy took another bite.

Bill looked up and caught Daisy watching him. "Why're you looking at me, Daisy Melon?"

She swallowed the popcorn in her mouth. "I told you not to call me that!" She knew he was making fun because Momma called her Daisy Punkin.

"That's your name, ain't it? Daisy Melon?"

Daisy doubled her fists. Anger rushed through her, and she wanted to punch Bill. "My name is Daisy Bovier Warren and you know it!" Daisy was proud that Momma had given her her maiden name as a middle name.

"Daisy Melon Warren," Bill said and giggled.

"Stop it, Bill," said Matt in a firm voice.

Bill shrugged and went back to his homework. He looked up the minute Matt wasn't watching and mouthed, "Daisy Melon."

Daisy grabbed his math paper and wadded it up into a tight ball and flung it across the room. "There!"

Bill jumped up. "You little brat!" He pushed her off her chair, and she landed with a painful thud on the floor.

"I hate you, Bill Warren!" Daisy burst into wild tears.

"Hey!" cried Matt. He picked up Daisy and

set her back on her chair before he faced Bill. "You will not be mean to your sister. Understand?"

"You tell him, Matt," said David with a chuckle.

Bill made a face at Matt. "She ruined my math paper! She's nothing but a baby brat!"

Daisy held her breath. Matt looked at her with his dark brows raised. She looked away at the balled paper on the floor.

"Go get it, Daisy," said Matt in a low, tight voice.

Daisy hesitated. She didn't want to mind Matt.

"Get the paper, Daisy," said Matt firmly.

She wanted to tell him to get it himself! But she remembered Momma's note. She sighed. Trembling, she walked to the paper. Her face burned fire red. She knew the boys were watching her. She wanted to scream at them to stop, but she bit her lower lip and kept quiet. She picked up the paper, smoothed it out, and held it out to Bill.

He grabbed it from her.

Matt sighed, but didn't say anything.

Daisy ran to her room and slammed her door shut. "Come home, Momma! Please, please come home! I don't want Matt to take care of me. I don't want to mind him."

She pulled out Momma's note and read it again. Her eyes widened. "The note doesn't say I have to mind Matt. It says Aunt Janet."

Daisy hugged Scruffy Punkin to her. "I just won't mind him after this if I don't want to!"

❤ ❤ ❤

Karen

8

With her head down so she wouldn't have to look at Matt, Daisy slowly walked into the kitchen. Last night Matt had tried to talk to her before she fell asleep, but she wouldn't talk. This morning he'd had to tell her three times to get out of bed and get dressed. Momma had always sat on the side of the bed and said,

"Daisy Punkin, you have to get up now and get ready for school. I have breakfast ready for you. Get up, my little sleepy head."

The third time Matt had said, "Get up right now, Daisy, or you'll go to school without breakfast."

She sat at her place at the table just as Bill dropped down across from her. Matt was eating a bowl of cereal in Dad's chair. Daisy frowned down at the table. There was no plate with french toast covered with margarine and syrup. There was no glass of chocolate milk. She scowled at Matt. "Where's my food?"

He smiled as if he hadn't seen her scowl. "The bowls are in the cupboard, the spoons in the drawer, and the boxes of cereal over there."

"I want Wheaties," Bill said.

"So do I," said Daisy. She ran to the box, grabbed it, and then peeked inside. "It's almost empty."

"I get it. I called it first." Bill grabbed the box from her, and she screamed and grabbed for it. He was taller and stronger than she, and she couldn't get it from him.

She stamped her foot and crossed her thin arms. "Give me the Wheaties right now, Bill! Matt, make Bill give me the Wheaties."

Matt shook his head. "Bill called Wheaties first, Daisy. You eat something else."

"I hate you, Matt!" she yelled. The terrible words stabbed through her. She saw the pain in Matt's eyes.

"You're spoiled rotten," snapped Bill as he poured milk in his bowl.

"You can't always have your own way, Daisy," Matt said gently. "It wouldn't be fair to the boys."

"Momma always lets her have her own way," said Bill.

Anger rose inside Daisy. She doubled her fists at her sides. "She does not!"

Bill pushed his face close to Daisy's. She smelled the toothpaste still on his breath. "She does too! She loves you more because you're a girl."

"Stop fighting, both of you," Matt said. He leaned back in his chair and studied Daisy until she wanted to scream at him again. "Daisy, it's time you stopped taking advantage of everyone just because you're the only girl. Jesus wants you to love your family."

Her stomach knotted, and she grabbed the box of cornflakes. Momma wanted her to learn about Jesus. But Momma said to learn from Aunt Janet, not from Matt.

Daisy ate her cornflakes in angry silence and wouldn't answer even when Matt asked her about school.

A few minutes later Daisy ran down the snowy walk toward the school and away from Matt. "Matt is not nice at all!" Her breath hung in the air. A gray car drove past with a red pickup close behind.

"Hey, Daisy! Wait up!"

Daisy turned to see Karen running toward her. She frowned, but waited. Cold wind blew into her hood. She stamped her feet to keep them from freezing inside her boots. Karen looked cold too. Her nose was bright red.

"I didn't know you lived near me," said Karen as she walked along beside Daisy.

"I live back there about half a block." Daisy pointed behind her.

"I live about two blocks that way."

"Did you find out who the dead woman was?"

"Yes." Karen rubbed the frayed cuff of her green jacket against her runny nose. "I never heard of her, but she lived in an apartment near us, Mom said. She had a fight with her boyfriend, and he stabbed her and dropped her off near our house. I saw the blood and every-thing. It was great!"

Daisy shuddered. "Did they catch the boyfriend and put him in jail?"

"Oh sure. I heard the sirens when they did. It was fun to watch it all. They handcuffed him and everything. I wanted to stay to watch, but my brother wouldn't let me. He says I see enough violence without being right there when it happens."

"I have *four* brothers." Daisy made a face.

"I have two brothers and a sister. Sometimes it's all right, but sometimes I wish I was an only child."

"Me too." Daisy thought about what Matt and Bill had said at breakfast. She frowned. She wasn't spoiled, and she didn't always get her own way. They were both mean.

Karen jumped over a crack in the sidewalk. "My mom's a beautician, and my dad works in a factory. What about yours?"

Daisy kicked at a clump of snow and sent it skittering ahead of her. "My dad puts in heat in new buildings and my . . . momma just stays . . . at home. She once worked as a waitress."

"What's wrong? Don't you like your mom?"

"I love her!" cried Daisy.

"Well, you looked funny when you were talking about her."

"I love her!"

"I didn't say you didn't."

"Oh." Daisy watched a gang of boys run across the schoolyard. "My momma had to go to Mississippi to stay with my grandma for two weeks. I miss her."

"I'd miss my mom if she was gone," said Karen.

"My cousin is taking care of us." Daisy made a face.

"I'm gonna be a policewoman when I grow up," Karen said with great pride in her voice. "What about you?"

Daisy shrugged. A car honked at the stop sign as several kids crossed the street.

Karen sniffed hard and rubbed her cuff across her nose again. "Mom says as much as I like violence I should be on the police force in a big city. Maybe Detroit. Grand Rapids is closer to home, though."

"Have you lived here long?"

"All my life."

Daisy looked at Karen in wonder. "I never lived in one place more than a year."

Karen scooped up a handful of snow,

packed it tight and round, and threw it against a tree. The snowball clung to the rough bark for a few seconds, then fell to the ground, leaving a crust of snow on the bark. "Want to work with me on the commercial for school?"

"I guess." She thought about Isaac. "Maybe Isaac can work with us."

"He wore a necktie to school once."

"I like him," said Daisy.

Karen shrugged. "I guess we could work with him."

"There he is now. Standing just outside the school." Daisy waved and Isaac waved back.

"Look at that red jacket he's wearing! It's another new one! I bet he has a whole closet of jackets." Karen looked down at her dirty, ragged jacket.

"He can't help it if he's rich," said Daisy.

"I guess not."

Isaac ran to them and smiled at Daisy. "Hi, Daisy." The smile vanished as he looked at Karen. "Hi."

"Hi," Karen said stiffly.

Daisy tugged at her red mittens.

"Daisy and I want you to work with us on the commercial we have to make. Want to?" asked Karen.

Isaac's face lit up, and then his shoulders drooped. "Are you teasing me again, Karen? Are you doing this so that in class you can say you won't have me in your group?"

"I know I did that for our science project, but I'm a Christian now, and I won't be mean anymore. Me and Daisy decided to let you work with us."

"Do you really want me, Daisy?" asked Isaac.

Daisy nodded.

"Then we'll be a team." Isaac squared his shoulders. "We'll make the best commercial in the class."

Daisy glanced away and thought about Momma. She didn't listen to the plans Isaac and Karen were making.

Would Momma be mad at her for being so mean to Matt?

❤ ❤ ❤

The Commercial

9

*T*hursday Daisy glanced at Miss Liscomb as she talked with some of the students at her desk. Long yellow hoop earrings almost brushed the shoulders of her yellow sweater when she moved her head. Daisy turned in her seat and looked back at the big wall map.

"Are you going to go to Mississippi?" whispered Isaac from his desk behind her.

"No."

He sighed in relief. "Good. I'd miss you."

Before she could say anything more, Miss Liscomb called the class to order and took roll. All morning Daisy watched the clock until finally it was time for Jason Silva to come talk about making commercials.

He walked into the room, and Miss Liscomb's face lit up. She smiled at him as if he were the only person alive. He took off his winter coat and draped it over a chair. He wore a bulky, loose-fitting red sweater with a red and white stripped shirt under it, and he had on black dress pants. His black shoes shone as if he'd polished them just before walking into the room. He ran his fingers through his curly brown hair. His blue eyes twinkled as he looked out at the students. To her surprise Daisy found herself smiling back at him.

Miss Liscomb motioned for him to follow

her around her desk to stand in front of it. Daisy liked the way Miss Liscomb's black and yellow skirt swirled around her legs as she walked. She was almost as tall as Jason Silva.

"Class, this is Jason Silva. Mr. Silva was kind enough to take time from his busy work schedule to come here today to talk to us about TV commercials." Miss Liscomb pushed the sleeves of her yellow sweater up and smiled. "Take all the time you want, Jason."

Daisy locked her hands in her lap and waited. She listened as he told about creating a commercial for the local furniture store as well as some of the businesses in Grand Rapids. His voice sounded like Matt's. She quickly pushed thoughts of Matt away.

"How many of you have seen the Tom Janeck's Auto Sales commercial?" asked Mr. Silva.

Daisy lifted her hand with several others.

"Did you like it?" asked Mr. Silva.

"Yes!" they all shouted at once.

"Good. I didn't write it, but it's a good commercial anyway." They all laughed, and when it was quiet again he continued, "You remember it because it makes you laugh. A good commercial will create an emotion in you that will make you remember the product advertised. So, that's what you're going to do. You'll find something to advertise, and you'll make your audience happy or sad or even angry. If you can get the audience to respond in some way, then you've made a good commercial that will sell the product."

To her surprise Daisy felt excitement bubbling up inside her. She was actually looking forward to making a commercial. Maybe she'd produce commercials when she grew up. It felt funny to think so far ahead. She had never before thought about what she'd do when she grew up.

After Jason Silva left, Miss Liscomb said, "Now, we'll divide into six groups and talk about the commercials we want to make. Here are the leaders of the groups: Isaac, Alison, Peter, Justin, Samantha, and Tara."

Isaac's hand shot up.

"Isaac?"

"May Daisy and Karen and Greg be in my group?"

"Yes," said Miss Liscomb.

Daisy sat back with a satisfied smile as the other leaders chose their groups. She glanced around to see if she could remember who Greg was, but she couldn't.

A few minutes later Daisy met with Isaac, Greg, and Karen in the corner near the book shelves. She sat cross-legged on the floor close enough to them that one knee touched Karen and the other Isaac. Greg sat across from her, but close enough that she could smell the gum he was chewing.

"We have a great idea for our commercial," said Isaac.

"For bug spray," said Greg with a laugh that made his white teeth flash in his black face. "We could make it real funny. One of us could be dressed like a can of spray and the others like bugs. The spray can would chase the bugs around and spray them. The bugs would drop over dead on their backs with their arms and feet in the air." They all giggled helplessly.

"That is funny," said Karen.

"I'll be a bug," said Daisy. Just then she realized that she hadn't thought about Momma since Jason Silva had walked in. A great sadness welled up inside her. She ducked her head and blinked hard.

"What's wrong, Daisy?" asked Isaac.

"Nothing," she whispered.

"You look sad again," he said.

Karen leaned over and looked into Daisy's face. "You're crying!"

Daisy sniffed.

Karen whispered, "Want me to pray for you?"

Daisy gasped in shock.

Karen laughed. "Hey, don't faint, Daisy. I know how to pray. Me and Isaac and Greg and some of the other kids do."

"That's right. We do," said Isaac.

Greg nodded. "We love Jesus. We know He wants to take away your sadness and make you happy."

"He does," said Isaac.

Daisy rubbed her hand over her eyes. Did Jesus really want to help her? "I don't know how to pray."

"We could teach you," said Karen. She wrinkled her nose. "Sometimes I don't act like Jesus wants me to because I haven't been a Christian very long. Sometimes I forget."

"Yeah, she does," said Isaac.

"But I do know how to pray," said Karen softly.

Daisy looked at the patch on her jeans. She had never met any kids her age that knew Jesus enough to know how to pray for others. Maybe she should ask them to tell her about Jesus. That way she wouldn't have to listen to Matt. Abruptly she pushed thoughts of Matt away. "Maybe you can pray for me later."

Just then the recess bell rang. Daisy jumped up and ran to get her jacket and boots.

Outdoors Alison walked up to Daisy. Alison smiled. "Hi."

"Hi." Daisy backed away.

"Making commercials will be fun, won't it?"

Daisy nodded.

Alison lifted her chin and looked very smug. "Our group has the best commercial idea. I bet you don't have even one idea."

"We do too! We're going to do one on bug spray. One person will be the can of spray, and the rest of us will be bugs." Daisy knew she sounded very smug too as she told the rest of the idea.

Alison smiled. "Hey, that does sound good."

"I know."

Alison leaned closer to Daisy and said, "You're new, so I'm going to help you. You don't know about Karen."

Daisy pushed her hands into her pockets and hunched her shoulders against the cold wind. She knew she wouldn't believe anything Alison said. "What about Karen?"

"You don't want to be friends with her." Alison looked around, then back at Daisy. "She's weird."

"Oh?"

"And she's a tomboy. And always dirty. She never brushes her hair." Alison pushed her long brown hair over her shoulder. "I could ask Miss Liscomb to take you off Isaac's group and put you on mine. As long as you never wear that dumb pink dress again. I could give them Leroy."

Daisy doubled her fists at her sides. "I'll stay with my group."

Alison lifted her chin. "Don't say I didn't warn you."

"I won't."

Alison pushed her face close to Daisy's. "I thought I just might like you, but I don't think I will."

Daisy lifted her chin. "I don't care."

Alison's mouth dropped open. "You don't care?"

"No."

Alison rubbed her mittens down her jacket. "But everyone wants to be my friend. I am the most popular girl in third grade."

"So?"

"Don't you ever try to be my friend again, new girl!" Alison spun around and ran off.

From behind Daisy Karen asked, "Did you make her mad?"

Daisy turned. "I guess so."

"She thinks she's so great. But she's just a spoiled brat. She's the only girl at her house, and she always gets her own way. I don't like her."

Daisy flushed. What if Karen learned that she always got her own way at her house? Would Karen call her spoiled too?

Was she spoiled?

Daisy didn't want to think about that.

❤ ❤ ❤

The Fight

10

Daisy slipped into the school. Recess wasn't over yet, but she wanted to look at the map again when no one was around. Cigarette smoke drifted out from the teachers' lounge. Piano music came from the kindergarten room.

Daisy stopped outside the third grade

room. She heard voices from inside. Carefully she peeked around the door. Alison stood with Miss Liscomb. Alison's face was bright with excitement.

"So, do you like our idea, Miss Liscomb? Can we use it?"

Miss Liscomb smiled and nodded. "Dressing like bugs and a can of bug spray is very original. You may use that for your commercial."

Daisy clamped her hand over her mouth to keep back a cry.

Alison flipped back her long hair. "What if someone else has the same idea?"

"They won't be able to use it," said Miss Liscomb. "The reason I asked each leader to tell me his group's idea was to keep from copying each other."

Daisy's heart zoomed to her feet. Her head spun. She'd told Alison their wonderful idea! Alison had stolen it!

Slowly Daisy walked down the hall toward

the outside door. How could she tell Isaac and Karen and Greg what she'd done?

Just as she touched the cold wide bar to open the door Alison called, "Hey, new girl, guess what?"

Anger rushed through Daisy. Her face burned. She waited for Alison. Suddenly she lunged at Alison and sent her sprawling to the snow-tracked tile floor.

"Get off me!" shouted Alison, shoving against Daisy. "You're crazy!"

"You stole our idea!" screamed Daisy. "I heard you!"

"Let me up!" Alison squirmed harder.

Strong hands gripped Daisy and she screamed. She looked around to find the principal, Mr. Moser. He lifted her off Alison. "What's the meaning of this, girls?"

Alison said, "She was trying to kill me!"

"I was not!" cried Daisy.

"Into my office, both of you." Mr. Moser pointed toward his office. His long coat flapped about his thin legs. His gray hair was mussed, and a piece of snow clung to his hollow cheek. "I can't believe big girls like you fighting like cats and dogs."

"It was her fault!" Daisy jabbed a finger at Alison.

"I didn't do anything! And you know it!" Alison looked very innocent. Daisy wanted to sock her in the eye.

A few minutes later, Daisy sat in a yellow plastic chair beside Alison and across the desk from Mr. Moser.

Mr. Moser made a tent of his thin hands and looked over them at the girls. "I will not tolerate that kind of behavior. Alison, you know that. Daisy, you're new, but I'm sure you know better."

Alison sniffed. "It was all her fault."

Daisy bit her lip and didn't say anything. She picked at a thread on her sweater cuff.

Mr. Moser cleared his throat. "Now, suppose you tell me what your fight was all about."

Alison jumped up. "I was walking out the door, and *she* jumped on me. I wasn't doing anything but walking out the door."

Daisy leaned back, her mouth open and her eyes wide.

"Daisy?" said Mr. Moser.

Daisy took a deep breath. "She stole our idea for a commercial."

Alison shook her head and looked even more innocent. "No, I didn't. Ask Miss Liscomb. I was the first person to tell her our idea for a commercial."

Daisy jumped up. "You're lying!"

"Daisy!" snapped Mr. Moser. "Both of you sit down and speak quietly. I'll call Miss Liscomb and get to the bottom of this." He glanced toward the door. "There she is now." He stepped out of his office and called, "Miss Liscomb, may I speak with you?"

Alison bumped Daisy's foot with hers. Daisy glanced at her, and Alison mouthed, "I hate you."

Daisy stuck her tongue out at Alison.

Mr. Moser and Miss Liscomb talked quietly just outside the doorway. Daisy's heart sank when she heard Miss Liscomb tell Mr. Moser that Alison had been the first to tell her the idea for a commercial.

Alison laughed a low laugh and nudged Daisy again.

Daisy locked her hands in her lap and pressed her lips tightly together.

Mr. Moser walked back to his desk. "I am going to punish both of you for fighting. Daisy, you cannot go out for recesses for the next three days. I'll inform your teacher of the punishment. Alison, you must stay in at noon hour and recess today."

"That's not fair!" cried Daisy.

"Don't make it harder on yourself, Daisy."

Impatiently Mr. Moser waved them out.

Daisy's face felt on fire. She walked toward her classroom with her fists doubled at her sides.

"Ha ha," said Alison in a low voice.

Daisy glared at her, but didn't speak. She walked to her desk and sat with her head down. Miss Liscomb hadn't called the class to order yet.

"What happened?" whispered Isaac.

Daisy slowly turned in her seat. Oh, she didn't want Isaac to know what she'd done, but she had to tell him. When she finished, she said, "I'm really sorry."

Isaac's eyes flashed with anger. "Alison is mean. She always does mean things."

"What'll we do?" asked Daisy.

Isaac motioned for Karen and Greg to join them. Then he told them what had happened.

Karen narrowed her eyes and glared at Alison's back.

"We could beat her up after school," said Daisy. She had heard her brothers talk about beating kids up, but she'd never done it before. Knocking Alison down was the only fight she'd ever been in.

Greg nodded. "Let's do it!"

"We can't," said Isaac.

"Why not?" asked Karen.

"Why not?" asked Daisy.

"Jesus doesn't want us to," replied Isaac. "He wants us to love our enemies and do good to them."

Daisy couldn't believe her ears.

"We won't even yell at Alison," said Isaac.

"I will," said Karen.

"Me too," said Daisy.

Isaac shook his head. "You'll just get into trouble. Jesus says to forgive her. He knows best."

Tears stung Daisy's eyes. How could Isaac be so nice? She looked at Greg and Karen. They both finally nodded in agreement. Jesus really did make a difference in the way people acted! Could he make a difference in her family like Momma had hoped?

❤ ❤ ❤

Daisy's Decision

11

*I*t was after school on Friday. Daisy took a deep breath and walked into the kitchen. Matt sat at the table reading. She almost turned and walked out. But she thought about Jesus and decided to stay. The smell of hot chocolate sent a hunger pang through her.

Matt smiled at her. "Hi, Daisy. You're a precious girl."

"I am?"

"You are! And I love you."

Daisy opened her eyes wide. "You do? But you yell at me all the time."

Matt reached out for her, and she let him pull her close to his side. "I didn't really yell, did I? But because I love you I won't let you be spoiled and always get your own way. I know you don't want to be selfish. Jesus wants to fill your heart full of love for others."

Tears stung her eyes, and she put her face against Matt's shoulder. All the way home from school again today she'd thought about getting to know Jesus like Karen and Isaac and Greg did. Even like Matt did.

"Jesus loves you, Daisy," Matt said softly.

"Are you sure?"

"Yes. The Bible says so. Remember I showed it to you the other day."

She nodded. She touched Matt's bright

sweater. Finally she said, "I want Jesus to be in me like He is in you."

Matt held her close. "We'll talk to Him right now."

Daisy listened as Matt prayed for Jesus to be her friend and Savior and Lord."

"Now you talk to Jesus, Daisy. Tell Him that you're sorry for the bad things you've done. Ask Him to forgive you. Tell Him to come fill your heart with His love."

She took a deep breath and said, "Jesus, I want You to fill my heart with love just like Matt's. Forgive me for being bad so many times. I am sorry! I want to love my brothers and my dad. I want to forgive Alison at school even if she is mean to me."

Deep inside Daisy felt a bubble of warmth burst and spread through her. "I do love You, Jesus. Thank You for loving me."

She pulled back from Matt and laughed through her tears. "Is Jesus my friend and Savior and Lord now?"

"Yes." Matt nodded and smiled. "You are

no longer the old Daisy Bovier Warren. You are a new little girl in Christ."

"Is God my Heavenly Father now?"

"Yes."

"And I can talk to Him and He'll answer?"

"Yes."

She thought about Momma and she smiled. "I want Momma to know Jesus too."

Matt wiped a tear off Daisy's cheek. "Your mom talked to my mom about God. She wanted to know Him. She also wanted Mom to teach her how to make her family a better family."

"And did Aunt Janet tell her?"

"Yes. Your mom said she'd study her Bible while she's in Mississippi." Matt pushed Daisy's hair behind her ears. "She said she'd also study a book that Mom sent her a while back on raising kids in a Christian home."

"What is a Christian home like, Matt?"

He smiled and tapped the end of her nose. "You'd like it. It's full of love. That doesn't mean we don't make mistakes and fight sometimes, but we always know that Jesus is there to help us get along and help us forgive and keep on loving."

Daisy looked down at the tips of Matt's sneakers, then up into his face. "Do you even love your dad and your brothers?"

He nodded.

"I don't know if I could love mine."

"You can. Jesus filled you with His love. And His love is big enough even for your dad and brothers."

She frowned thoughtfully. If Matt said it was true, she knew it had to be, but she just couldn't imagine loving them like she loved Momma. She smiled at Matt. "I'll help you fix supper, Matt."

"Thanks." He hugged her close. "You can unload the dishwasher." He walked toward the stove and then stopped and stood with his hands resting lightly on his lean hips. "Want a cup of hot cocoa first?"

"Sure." She took a flowered mug from the cupboard and handed it to him.

He poured cocoa into it and handed it back to her.

"Thanks." She leaned against the counter and sipped it. It was hot and sweet. "It's yummy, Matt."

He winked at her and then boosted himself up on the counter.

"Daisy, I've learned something the past few days."

"What?"

"It's not easy cleaning house and doing the washing and the cooking. And the grocery buying with only a few dollars to spend. I helped with the work at home, but I never had to do it all." He looked around the kitchen. "It's a lot of work! Today I called Mom and told her how much I appreciate how hard she works to keep the house nice and the family fed. She laughed and said it was about time I appreciated her." He kissed the top of Daisy's head. "So, Daisy, when your momma comes home, you appreciate her."

"I will!" And she'd try hard not to act like a

spoiled brat. She finished the cocoa and then unloaded the silverware. Her head whirled with the thought of Momma coming home. Suddenly she realized that Momma really was coming home when she was finished at Nana's. The fear that had filled her since Momma had left was all gone. She was free to be happy. It was all right to think of other things — other things like the commercial they were doing in school.

She walked to the table where Matt sat. "Matt?"

"Yes?" He looked up from reading the cookbook.

"We're producing commercials at school, and I have to meet with the kids that I'm working with. Can they come here so we can plan together?"

"Sure. When?"

She glanced at the clock. "Now."

Matt nodded. "What're you doing your commercial on?"

"I don't know yet."

Just then someone knocked at the front door, and Daisy ran to answer it. Isaac and Karen stood there. Cold air rushed in. "Come in," Daisy said, stepping back.

"Greg couldn't come," said Karen. "His dad said he had too many chores. But he'll be able to work with us tomorrow."

Isaac dropped his jacket on a chair with Karen's. "Greg said if he thought of a brilliant idea he'd call and tell us."

Just then Daisy heard the neighbor's dog bark. An idea popped into her head. She laughed. "How about a dog food commercial? Three of us will be dogs, and one can be the one who talks about it."

"The narrator," said Isaac.

"We'll line up dishes of dog food, and the dogs will only go to the food we're trying to sell," said Karen. "They'll fight over it."

"And then a cat will come in and scare the dogs away and eat the food," said Daisy with a laugh.

"That's great!" cried Isaac and Karen together.

"Two of us will be dogs," said Isaac, "one a cat, and the other the narrator."

Daisy beamed with pride. She'd lost their other commercial. Now she'd thought up a new one. "This time I won't tell anyone, especially not Alison," she said.

She waited for anger at Alison to stab her, but nothing happened. She smiled.

"I smell hot cocoa," said Karen, sniffing.

"Come to the kitchen and meet my cousin Matt," Daisy said. "And we'll have hot cocoa while we work."

A Noise in the Kitchen

12

Daisy sat up in bed with a start. The tiny night light in the hallway still glowed, so she knew it was the middle of the night. She frowned. What had made her wake up? It was Monday, but she didn't have to get up until seven. Yesterday Daddy had let her and the boys go to Sunday school and church with Matt. She couldn't wait to tell Isaac and Karen and Greg.

She crept to the hallway. The only sound was Jim's snoring. Sometimes he snored so loud that she shut the boys' bedroom door just so she wouldn't hear it. Sometimes she'd still hear him, so she'd put her pillow over her head.

She tugged at her warm flannel pajamas as she tiptoed to the living room. A street light spilled light into the living room, and she saw Matt sleeping on the couch.

She stood beside the couch, looking down at Matt. He lay on his side, his head half buried in his pillow, his breathing regular. Should she wake him and tell him she was awake?

Just then she heard a noise from the kitchen. Her stomach tightened. Maybe Bill hadn't been able to go to sleep after Matt had scolded him for making fun of their dog food commercial. Friday and Saturday Bill had watched them practice the commercial without saying anything. Then last night when she'd practiced being the cat, he'd said, "Can't you think up a better commercial? Yours is dumb. It'll be the worst one in all of third grade."

Daisy shivered just thinking about how angry Bill had been at Matt for sending him to his room.

Was Bill in the kitchen pouting all alone?

Daisy tiptoed across the living room, careful of the spot beside Momma's favorite chair that creaked when someone stepped on it.

The light over the stove was on. It bathed the kitchen in a soft glow. Bill wasn't there. Dad was. Daisy almost turned and ran back to her room. But she stood in the doorway without making a sound. She smelled the popcorn that Jim had made while they watched TV before bedtime. She heard Dad moan.

He sat at the table in Momma's place, his back hunched, his hands over his face. He wore a black tee shirt and jeans and his feet were bare.

Was he crying?

Daisy had never seen him like this before. Dare she speak to him? Maybe she should run back to bed and pretend she'd never seen him. She turned to leave, then stopped. He looked sad and alone. How could she walk away? Silently she asked Jesus to give her the courage to talk to Dad.

Slowly she walked to the table. The faded linoleum felt cold against her bare feet. Finally she whispered, "Daddy?"

His head shot up, and he frowned. Tears stood in his blue eyes. His face was dark with whiskers. "What're you doing out of bed?" he snapped.

"I woke up."

"Well, get right back where you belong."

She took half a step toward him, her heart pounding. "Momma will come home soon, and then you'll feel better."

"And what if she doesn't come back?"

"She will. She's only helping Nana. I know she'll be back."

"You sound so sure."

She nodded. "I am."

Dad shuddered and rubbed an unsteady

hand across his eyes. "I don't know where I went wrong. Once she loved me, and now she don't."

Daisy touched his arm. "She loves you, Daddy."

"I don't know how she can. I'm no good. No good for her or for any of you. And you all know it."

"Oh, Daddy." She wanted to put her arms around him, but she couldn't. Maybe she should wake Matt up so he could talk to Dad. Matt would know what to say. But she didn't move.

"Go to bed, Daisy. I'll be all right."

She laced her fingers together. "It makes me feel bad to see you sad."

"Yah, me too." He stabbed his slender fingers through his hair. "She says I'm a gypsy. Always on the move. She says I'm running from myself. If I stayed in one place long enough to have time to relax, I might have to deal with what I've become."

"What have you become?"

He rubbed his hand across his face, and his whiskers sounded raspy. "A hard person to live with."

Daisy couldn't remember him any other way.

"When David and Jim were small, we did things together. Went on vacations together. I played with them. I laughed with them."

"What happened to you?"

"I don't know. I've been trying to sort it all out."

Daisy licked her dry lips. "Jesus loves you, Daddy."

"I used to think so."

"He does. The Bible says so."

"Does that make it true, Daisy?"

"Yes." She nodded. "Yes."

He nodded. "That's what my sister Janet told me, but that seems like too simple of an answer."

"Not to me. Jesus hears when we talk to Him, and He helps us with our problems. Matt told me."

"Oh." Dad scowled. "Matt."

"Don't you like him at all?"

"He makes me mad. He walks in here and takes over, and nobody even misses your mom."

"I do! Bill does! He told me. The other boys do too."

Dad shook his finger at Daisy. "You kids mind Matt more than you did your momma."

Daisy hung her head. "I know. And I'm sorry."

"You should be!"

"Matt makes us mind, and Momma didn't very much." Daisy lifted her chin and squared her shoulders. "But I'm not going to act spoiled any longer. I am going to help Momma all I can so she's not our slave. I'll mind her without fighting. I mean it too! Jesus will help me."

"She says she needs my help to raise you kids." Dad spread his hands in a helpless gesture. "What do I know about raising kids? I can't even raise myself."

Daisy hunted for something to say, but couldn't find anything.

Dad looked at her strangely. "Do you know this is the first time I ever talked to you?"

She nodded. "Yes. I know."

"I'm so sorry, Daisy!"

"That's okay. I forgive you."

"You must hate me!"

"I don't." She looked right into his blue eyes that matched her own. "Jesus helped me love you."

"Did He?"

"Yes. He'll help you love me too."

"Do you think I could give you a hug?" Dad whispered hoarsely.

Daisy hesitated, then nodded.

Dad wrapped his arms around her and held her. It felt strange, but nice. She could smell the sweaty tang of his skin and hear the beat of his heart. Finally he released her, and she stepped back, her cheeks red with embarrassment. "Run on to bed, Daisy. You got to get up for school in a couple of hours. You're doing your commercial, aren't you?"

"Not until Tuesday. I'm the cat, and I chase

Karen and Greg away from the dog food. Isaac's the narrator." Daisy giggled just thinking about the fun they'd have performing the commercial for the class. "I wish you could see it, Daddy."

"Me too, but I have to work."

"I know." It made her feel good just to know he wanted to see it.

"Go on to bed now."

She nodded.

"I'll be all right," he said.

"You sure?"

"Yes. Good night . . . Daisy Punkin," he whispered.

"Good night, Daddy." She smiled, then turned, and ran to her room and stopped just inside.

Daddy had talked to her! He had even called her Momma's pet name for her! Daisy dabbed a tear off her cheek. In a few days Momma would be home, and she'd ask, "You been a good girl, Daisy Punkin?"

And she'd say, "Sure have, Momma. I love you, Momma. So does Jesus. And so does Daddy."

Daisy picked up Scruffy Punkin and hugged him tight. "Daddy talked to me. He even hugged me, Scruffy Punkin. He really did."

Some day she might get used to it. Maybe it wouldn't be hard for Daddy to make the changes Momma had said he needed to make. Jesus would help him.

Daisy touched her hair where he had touched it and rubbed her hand along her arm where his arms had been.

Slowly she climbed into bed and pulled the covers to her chin. She closed her eyes. "Heavenly Father, thank You for my daddy. And Momma. And even Bill and Ron and Jim and David. Thank You that Matt came to stay with us and teach us to love You."

Suddenly Daisy giggled. "And thank You for helping me to be the best cat in the whole world for our commercial Tuesday."

Daisy turned on her side, hugged Scruffy Punkin tight, and fell fast asleep.

♥ ♥ ♥